INSECT DREAMS

INSECT DREAMS

Rosalind Palermo Stevenson

▲
Rain Mountain Press
New York City

Copyright© 2007 by Rosalind Palermo Stevenson

All rights reserved. No part of this book may be reproduced or transmitted in any form or by any means, electronic or mechanical, including photocopy, recording, or any information storage and retrieval system, without permission in writing from the publisher.

INSECT DREAMS was originally published in the 2003 anthology *Trampoline (Small Beer Press)*.

For permission to make copies of any part of this work, contact: rpstevenson@aol.com

ISBN: 0-9786105-2-0

Text set in Tiffany
Designed by Sarah McElwain
First Edition

Printed in the United States of America

Library of Congress Cataloging-in-Publication Data

Stevenson, Rosalind Palermo.
  Insect dreams / Rosalind Palermo Stevenson. -- 1st ed.
    p. cm.
  ISBN 0-9786105-2-0
  1. Merian, Maria Sibylla, 1647-1717--Fiction. 2. Women naturalists--Fiction. 3. Insects--Fiction. 4. Suriname--Fiction. 5. Netherlands--Fiction. 6. Psychological fiction. I. Title.
  PS3619.T4928I57 2007
  813'.6--dc22
                        2007018241

*For my grandmothers,
Julia and Mary.*

ACKNOWLEDGMENTS

The author gratefully acknowledges the following:

The anthology, *Trampoline,* (edited by Kelly Link, Small Beer Press), where "Insect Dreams" was originally published.

The National Museum of Women in the Arts' Library and Research Center in Washington, DC for their generous assistance when I was researching Maria Sibylla Merian's life and work, and for their continued assistance in granting permission to use her artwork.

The Pierpont Morgan Library and Museum in New York City where I first discovered Maria Sibylla Merian and her "*Dissertation in Insect Generations and Metamorphosis in Surinam.*"

The authors of the many books on a vast array of subjects which I consulted as part of my research for this novella. Special acknowledgment is made to Natalie Zemon Davis' *Women on the Margins: Three Seventeenth Century Lives.*

Special thanks to Luna Tarlo for her insightful reading and willingness to enter my world.

Many thanks also to Patricia Duffy, Kathryn Ugoretz, and Ruth Lamborn for their early reading and encouragement.

I

... and then the sounds begin to reach her, the violent beating of wings, a breeze rising up, a bird gliding on wing... a vision of mouths, footsteps on the gravel on the walkway, the kicking up of stones, the shifting weight from left to right, vibrating deep into the earth, and moving past... a vision of something sweet, of something sugary, or of a soft secretion, she is folded in upon herself, like a leaf which has fallen and curled... a vision of the garden's weedy waters, of its ghostly portico, its statues, the Dutch moat, a sunflower, roses and other flowers... a vision, a vision, the cry of a bird again, on wing nearer now, furious spasms in her abdomen, the bird on wing higher, higher, then out of view... a vision of longing, a burning up, a flap of skin to which she must affix herself, to which she must hold fast, hold fast, there is a high wind coming, there is the danger she will be blown away...

Sometime in the night a sound wakes her: a thud as of a heavy object falling, and then someone moaning. Maria Sibylla Merian sits up, but can hear nothing more. The night is long, too long, and the air is stultifying. Down in the hold of the ship the insect moth, *Phalaena tau*, is dreaming, day or night, it makes no difference, though now it is night. The moth is in chrysalis with the other specimens that Maria Sibylla has brought with her on the journey.

Awake she finds she cannot breathe, her cabin is airless, and the odor is foul even here at the stern so close to the captain's quarters. She comes up to the deck to breathe the air, in the dead of night, alone, a forbidden female figure, solitary, silent, and all the while the ocean reticent, the waves just barely lapping.

Imagine. Imagined. The fragmentary themes that drive her night. The ocean. The Atlantic. The crossing to Surinam. It is an allegorical crossing like the crossings of Moors. The dark faces of the men. The ship, The Peace, just barely rocking.

She recalls the ritual dances of certain insects. The way the female becomes bloated and huge. And gives off an odor that is strong and pungent, but at the same time sweet, and the males pick up the scent and approach, half-flying, half-crawling, to the female.

Now she stands on the deck of the ship. Induced by her God. Under the ceiling of Heaven. Beneath the planets and the stars. The constellations—Lepus, Monoceros, Eridanus. Love of knowledge. Travel and changes. Danger of accidents (especially at sea). And a danger of drowning.

Heavenly God, it is Your will that guides me. It is Your will that guides the entire universe, that binds all forms together. Heavenly God, take me into that self-same will and guide me to Your perfection.

Does she know Plato's Sea of Tartarus? Where all the waters pierce the earth to the Sea of Tartarus?

The sailors believe that if they come too close to the equator they will turn black like the natives who live there. Or that if they sail too far to the north their blood will congeal and turn to ice in their veins. But tonight there is nothing but the black of black waters, the sea of darkness, the stars in the heavens.

Pale woman. Defined by your sex. By your birth. By your birth right. When did the door first open? It was her father's influence, no doubt, the artist Matthäus Merian the elder. She was a child when he died and her memory of him is imperfect. Papa. Papa Matthäus. The safe, the clean, the eminently sane smell of him.

She holds the cast of the head of Laocoon.
Observe the way she holds the giant head.
Sirs, I hold this head, the head of poor Laocoon who warned against the Trojan horse.
She is exceptional, her father tells the men.
Stand over here, Maria Sibylla, over here, stand and hold the head.
It is a plaster cast and heavy for a small child; it weighs at least seven or eight pounds, but she holds it.
She holds it as though it is not heavy, as though it does not weigh seven or eight pounds.

and the canals below the windows

the dead level of the waters

the canals that one can see in all directions

It is the light reflecting on her cup of liquid. A small plate next to it with crumbs. It is one of the mornings in the Netherlands before she makes her ocean crossing. A child brings her insects from the Kerkstraat Gardens. It is a ritual they perform: the child arrives at the door and calls out to the woman, "Mistress."

    Ja, what have you brought?
    I brought a moth pupa.
    Did you pluck it yourself?
    Yes, Mistress.
    Where did you find it?
    I found it in the Kerkstraat Gardens.
    Here, come, let me see.
    The child, a girl, holds out the inert, brown shell of the pupa.
    Ja, I see, rolling it delicately over on the palm of her hand.
    The child's eye is becoming sharp, a love for precision is developing, a satisfaction in identification of the insects. She is just one of the children who lives around the Kerkstraat Gardens, but Maria Sibylla has taken an interest in her.

    Maria. Maria Sibylla.

    Sibylla is the woman's middle name, the name passed down to her from her mother.

    And the Sibyl closed her eyes and saw events unfold before them, in the darkness a horse falling, its rider going down in battle, and then many horses falling, and many riders going down in battle, and rains, and plagues to cleanse the earth.

Make way, make way.

In Amsterdam it was all excitement and exotica. That was how the fire took hold inside her; it was from what she saw in Amsterdam, brought back by the science travelers. But they were hobbyists compared to her, compared to her deadly seriousness. The fire took hold from what she saw in Amsterdam in the interiors of the museum rooms. The creatures floating as in dreams. The creatures in their cases floating.

There are creatures that no one has ever seen. Creatures that have not been classified, counted, entered in the journals and the record books of science, whose shapes defy the patterns of logical construction, whose colors are as if from other worlds, self-regenerating, pure, infinite variety and complexity, sketched by God, painted by angels, life miraculously breathed into them, life, alive, free, that no one has seen, that she, she must see.

The air is cold on her face, cold through to her bones.

The night is bearing down on her and she thinks that it will crush her. The way the night bears down on her.

The night bears down and makes her think of dying oceans, of vast bodies of water slowly releasing and losing breath, and of all the life contained down in the oceans' depths, down in those fathomless deeps, and of all the life carrying on with the business of living, and with the business of feeding and mating and dying.

The air is cold on her face. Cold through to her bones. She is out from her cabin. Out on the deck. Wrapped in her folds of black twill.

The ship has slowed down almost to a standstill. There is no wind, light or moderate, no fresh and strong wind, no scant wind, no aft, no large, no quartering wind.

She is steady on the deck, steady on her feet, she has her sea legs, she can walk on them, she keeps her back straight.

The sailors will not look at her. They believe it will bring bad luck to look at her. They believe she is a witch—*die Hexe, bezaubernde Frau*.

She is a woman traveling alone under the protection of the captain, in her sight-line the insects of Surinam.

There will be land soon. She can smell it. It is a sweet smell in the air mingled with the smell of salt. Anticipation of arrival. The first rays of the sun. Thin and tentative. The slow lifting of the darkness.

Surinam. Soor i nam. State of the kingdom of the Netherlands on the North-east coast of South America. 55,144 square miles. Capital, Paramaribo.

Paramaribo. Delicious word. Sweet as the sugar cane that grows there, sweet and savage.

Birds tear towards the sun. Their wings on fire like the wings of the Holy Spirit. Tongues aflame for all the earth to see.

She wakes gasping for air, her body bathed in perspiration; her hair is pasted to her head by the perspiration. She pulls the bed sheets off her body, lifts into the mesh netting that envelops her bed, it is the mosquito netting, she lifts her face into it and it feels like a spider's web, the silky softness, the sensation of the light, thin fabric against her face. She thrusts her hands out in front of her, pushes the fabric away, remembers where she is, what this is, reaches into the blackness to find the seam and lifts away the netting. She locates the candle on her bedside table and lights it. Is guided by its sallow light to the window where she stands looking out, again the night, the moon a harsh orange sliver in the sky.

She is in the bedroom in her suite of rooms at Surimombo—Surimombo is the plantation-lodging house owned by the spinster, Esther Gabay. At the time of her stay, there are these three others: Francina Ivenes, the widow, a permanent lodger at Surimombo since the death of her husband some years ago; the physician, Doctor Peter Kolb, who has his practice in the township; and Mathew van der Lee, the young settler, who has come to profit in the sugar trade.

Surimombo. It is a chorus from the slaves. *The race to the end.* Surimombo. Surimombo. Monsoon rain, water washing down the Parima, the fabled river that ran through Paradise. It is the place that was Eden when God expelled Adam. And Eve had no choice but to follow. And now the Parima with its current, the way Maria Sibylla looks in the canoe, she looks large in the canoe, with her back straight, a giantess carrying her insects.

And from the river a disturbance, from deep down under the greenblue bowl of agitation and foment,

Surinam is all rivers: the Nickerie; the Saramacca; the Coppename and the Suriname; the Commewijne and the Marowijne; the Para; the Cottica; the Maroni; the Tapanahoni,

and all around the rolling fields of sugar cane, the way the stalk breaks so that the sweet pulpy insides come dripping out, inviting you to bite, to suck,

it is impossible not to bite, to suck, the rich sweetness.

The sun throws glints of light that catch from time to time the defensive pose of a pupa; still, still, breathless, nothing that moves, nothing that will give rise to movement. It looks like the dropping of a macaw, or like a piece of wood, a bit of broken twig, the pupa waiting to unfold.

It is at the end of the dry season and many times throughout the day she must wait before she can move on. She must take shelter and wait for the rain to stop.

The jungle forest is open to her, and she keeps step with its pace, with its drifting and continuous movement.

What looks like a centipede, or a snake curled on a branch, is nothing more than the branch itself, its curve, a thickness in the growth of its bark, a guest shrub growing in an enclave of its formation. Meanwhile the creature that she seeks is there, no more than an arm's length in front of her, its eyes focused in her direction.

She is with Marta, her Amerindian slave who seems hardly a slave at all, though one of a dozen slaves included in her lodging fees at Surimombo. Marta knows the names of the trees, the leaves and branches, the larvae feeding on them, the moths they will transform into. She knows the frogs, the spiders, the snakes, the birds, hummingbirds drinking the nectar of flowers, the buds, the fruits, macaws screaming in the trees, winged and magnificent, their colors streaming like the colors in flags, the flags of the homelands, the welcoming flags of homecomings.

Back in Amsterdam she has a friend, a woman who has grown a giant pineapple. From all around people have come to see it, and Mr. Caspar Commelin has written an article about it for inclusion in his science journal. Maria Sibylla writes to Caspar Commelin, and to the other Amsterdam naturalists, the men who are part of the scientific exchange.

Sirs, I have had the satisfaction this day, the 21st of January, 1700, to witness the transformation of a caterpillar, gold and black striped, which I found soon after my arrival here; to witness it become these months later, a butterfly.

She works in watercolors on vellum.

Her vellum is the finest there is, made from the skin of lambs, the lambs unborn, taken early, violently.

Suppers at Surimombo are served each evening at six o'clock. Esther Gabay takes her place at the head of the table. On the side to Esther Gabay's right are seated Doctor Peter Kolb and Mathew van der Lee. Maria Sibylla is seated opposite them, next to the Widow

Ivenes. The food is always plentiful and rich: large bowls of mutton and fricassees, platters of Guinea fowl and vegetables, mullets and snapper, fruits and tarts, alligator pears, guava and shaddock. Nut meats and oranges are brought to the table last, along with pastries dripping with sugar. The meal is served from left to right. The conversation is animated and jovial.

"How exotic your insects are," says the Widow Ivenes to Maria Sibylla. "Do they ever crawl upon your hand or on your wrist? What does it feel like when that happens—the sensation of the insects crawling on your flesh?"

Sirs, The quickening. Life appearing in the egg and nourished there. And then ferocious biting through. The pede, the stage at which I plucked it, plucking too the leaves on which it fed until its transformation into pupa. Profoundest rest. A rest that angels yearn for—and for that time asleep and dreaming. Then beckoned by the dream it starts to stir, the slightest stirring, and then a parting of the cotton that protects the shell, and a splitting and a chipping of the shell itself, until the transformation is complete from pede to winged creature; emerging, blasting, to fly dazed and free and glorious.

Out of a sky filled with sun, out of air that is still and filled with the scent of Flamboyant and sugar cane, storms rise up without warning and blacken the Surinam sky. A breeze begins to blow in the darkened light, a moist breeze that takes hold and the sweet smells are carried stronger, and the moisture in the air bathes the face; but then the breeze gathers strength and becomes a wind, and the wind a raging gale, and the gale gains hurricane force. There are signs if one takes notice. Everything becomes quiet. There is a cessation of the sounds of the birds and the insects.

Maria Sibylla is out behind the Surimombo plantation house when her first storm forms in the stillness. She is studying a species of potter wasp which has built its nest upon the ground. She is intent upon recording her observation and writing the notes that will accompany her drawings; she does not take notice of the darkening light. It is Mathew van der Lee who comes running to fetch her—frantic his running, shouting something she cannot hear, stopping just short of knocking into her, he grabs her sketching papers and her charcoals, and though now quite on top of her, he continues his shouting. They are not back inside the house five minutes when the walls begin to rattle, and the whistling of the wind becomes deep and throaty like a lion's roar, and she huddles low with Esther Gabay, and with the Widow Ivenes and Doctor Peter Kolb, and with Mathew van der Lee, she huddles low.

The storm subsides and the sounds start up again, the rasp of insects, the calls of birds, the screeching of monkeys.

Mathew van der Lee inquires if he might accompany Maria Sibylla on a collecting expedition she has planned to the shoreline in the aftermath of the storm. It is his speciality, the shoreline, he tells her; he had been a collector himself back in the Netherlands.

She packs her vellums and her charcoal, her nets and her collecting jars.

She walks erect and keeps her back straight, her shoes are caked with mud, the bottom of her skirt is wet and dragging.

It is light. The sun completely broken through. The hills behind the shore heavy with what the winds have brought, invisible but present, the air laden with it.

"Madame Sibylla," says Mathew van der Lee. He wears a hat in the style of the day, black felt and rimmed. He wears a jacket also in the style of the day, three quarters in length and black like the hat, and his shirt is white beneath the jacket. They are on the edge of the shoreline along the Paramaribo coast. Maria Sibylla is walking ahead of him. "Madame Sibylla," he says again. "You shall outdistance me if you walk so quickly, Madame Sibylla." He is teasing and young, pleasing and handsome in his white shirt, in his hat, in his jacket.

Sirs, we sing the creature's praises! The pede perceives the visual impressions around it, not by means of rows of eyes located down along the sides of its body, but through distinctly tiny simple eyes, ocelli, placed on each side of the head.

For a minute she is breathless. Her breathlessness exaggerated in the intensity of the heat. It is so hot she almost cannot bear it.

The Widow Ivenes beckons her to visit in her suite of rooms. The Widow is sitting with a metal plate against her forehead, alternately placing it against the back of her neck. The drapes are drawn. There is a bowl of water on the table by her bed. "I would like to tear these clothes from my body," the Widow says point blank to Maria Sibylla.
 Maria Sibylla has come into the Widow's room with a fan with which she is fanning herself unrestrainedly. It was hand-paint-

ed in Italy, but she purchased it in Amsterdam. She offers it as a present to the Widow Ivenes. The Widow takes the fan and heaves and sighs, and heaves and sighs again.

Only Esther Gabay seems to never mind the heat. She carries on in it with the running of Surimombo. Even during the hottest hours, she carries on in it, just as the slaves carry on in it with their work in the sugar fields.

The African slaves go about naked. Or mostly naked. The women naked from waist to neck. The young ones with their breasts taut, their skin the deepest browns, their nipples black, like black cherries on the trees back in Holland. The older women stand with their breasts below their waists in the late day sun. There is a dance the African slaves perform and Maria Sibylla has witnessed it—the Winti, or Dance of Possession—their hips roll as they pass the calabash, drink from the bowl, smoke the tobacco, and then *here Miss, here Miss,* holding out the worm for her to take, *here Miss, here Miss...*

That evening there is smoked salmon arrived by ship from Amsterdam. With the salmon is turtle and king fish, grouper and snapper. A beverage is served made of coconut and lime. Hands are washed between courses. The evening meal is like a prayer. Like a service in the church in Paramaribo.

late at night she hears the doctor snoring, she hears him through the walls of the suites of the house, his breath coming in snorts and gasps.

and in the eaves around the house—spiders.

and in her room the smell of the salve she uses to protect her skin. It is something Marta gave her made from the sap of palm leaves. And blood oranges in a bowl. And grapes in another bowl. Her hair is wrapped in cloth. The cloth is cut in strips and woven through her hair. Blood oranges in a bowl next to the grapes.

and what she feels is the heat. The relentless bruising heat.

Sirs, it has been thought the thickened lines of wing venation are veins like those that comprise the network of our own fragile bodies, and through which the moth's blood (made up of a dense white liquid) flows outward each to body parts dependent on receiving it. This proves not the case. The wing venation are solidly composed and act as brace cords for support.

She is in the small forest behind the Surimombo sugar fields. They call it Surimombo Forest because its edges border the plantation. The light is green and indistinct. Her eyes must make an adjustment. The light filters down through the branches of the trees, and through the flowers that grow along the tree trunks. A flatworm glides on a moist trail of sludge on the leaf of a giant acacia. The worm is red and iridescent. When she tries to lift it, it dissolves.

God stirs. In any case impels. Nettles. On which the creature feeds. The Mora branch. And its leaves. The Yucca with its red fruit.

Mathew van der Lee has followed her into the small forest where she is working along its edges. It was by chance, he says, that he caught sight of her, from the sugar fields where he had been observing the harvesting technique at Surimombo. He could not resist, he says, but to see after her, to inquire of her while at her work. I have seen many such plants in the botanical gardens in Amsterdam, he says, pointing to the crimson blossoms of the bougainvillaea, but none in the gardens compare to these.

It has been said that there were no lovers, only a husband who wound up by menacing—the rumors of his vices—and the whispers of the word cruelty—a husband whom she fled in retaliation and defense. A daring act then, at that time, imagine.

But history shall have it there was a lover.

Maria Sibylla is not a child. No. She is a woman already of some years. Though she was little more than a child on the day of her marriage to Johann Graff. But she fled that husband.

On the 21st day of November in the year 1685, Maria Sibylla gathered what was hers and set out for the Protestant Pietist colony at Freisland, and for the colony's home at the Castle of Weirweurd, and for the prefect, Petre Yvon, who then presided there. She set out to join those pious men and women who lived each moment in the love of God and in the denial of the worldly influence. She took her vellums, her charcoals, her specimens, some articles of clothing, some personal effects.

On the morning of the 23rd of November, her husband appeared outside the door of the Castle, where he bellowed out the name of his wife, and where within those walls Maria Sibylla remained silent.

She was staring out her window when he arrived, thinking of the creatures she might find there, wondering how she might conduct her work from this new home, she was seeing God in all she saw, and trusting in God to direct her.

Graff sought audience with his wife through the personage of Petre Yvon. He demanded that he be admitted inside the walls of the castle. She is mine, he shouted, mine, I will not let go what is rightfully mine.

Only silence for reply.

And though he went down in a rage on his knees and pounded on the rock strewn ground for three days, eating nothing, and not even drinking water, and though the ground was cold in the strong November chill, and though he made supplication and implored, and beseeched and importuned, and alternately begged and bellowed, she would not yield.

Tropical sweetness now. Sweeter than the sugar cane. Sweeter than the syrup dripping from the stalks cut and bound for refining. Blinding sun. Blazing heat. Leaves of plants so delicate they wither in the sun.

Sirs, the female is fussy in her decision as to where to lay her eggs; she grades each leaf for suitability, rejecting one leaf after another before choosing.

Insects swarm, approaching hungry and curious, the jungle forest stretches before her, sounds, the glimpses of birds. She is on her way to Rama, farther down along the Saramacca. The African slaves walk ahead of her, unsheathing knives flashing, cutting a path through the dense growth of the forest, hacking down the weeds and the sawgrass so she can pass through. She has with her bottles half-filled with brandy to preserve dead some of what she finds, but also the mesh cages lined with bolting cloth to take other specimens alive, and to retain for them the natural conditions of their environment, to study their transformations without interrupting them, to observe for herself all the stages of their development. Her head is covered with a wide-brimmed hat. A few beads of perspiration run down from beneath the hat. She wears a shirt under the makeshift overall that she has sewn for her work in the jungle. The Surimombo slaves call her medicine woman. The women bring her chrysalids that they promise will open into moths, and butterflies more beautiful than any she has ever seen, creatures that will whisper certain truths to her, endow her with certain powers. But everything now has begun to draw her attention. It is no longer simply the larvae, the moths and the butterflies. Now she wants to know frogs, toads, snakes, and spiders, hummingbirds, the parrots and red monkeys screeching in the trees, the habits of the grasses that grow here, the invisible creatures that inhabit the air.

Sirs, for each there is the head, the thorax, the abdomen; the surface of the body divided into plate-like areas; there are the mouth parts, the antennae, the feet; and the special hairs that are sensitive to sound.

"Your hands are so delicate, Dear," the Widow Ivenes tells Maria Sibylla that night at supper, "one would never guess from looking at them you are a scientist."

Pastries and puddings are brought to the table, jellies and preserved fruits, fruit tarts sitting in transparent syrups, cakes made from nut meats, sweet oranges, yellow pineapples, alligator pears, guava, shaddock.

After supper Mathew van der Lee asks permission to enter Maria Sibylla's study. It is in a ground floor room at the rear—attached to, but distant from the other rooms of Surimombo. "Mr. van der Lee, Here, come." Before he is able to say a word, he is directed to a brownish shape in a mesh cage that looks at first as though it might be a curled bit of bark. But then there is the slightest movement. A kind of weaving from side to side, a tear in the wall at one end, a small but violent movement, the tear opening a little larger, and then a little larger still, until a shape is visible inside, pushing forward through the tear, a damp and matted little thing pushing its way through the opening until it has pushed itself fully out, and then sits and rests there for a time. "There, you see," is all she says.

Sirs, There is a heart, as well, I have found it lodged in the frontal vessel suspended from the wall of the abdomen. The tiny heart can almost not be seen. But it is, I assure you, there, and it does beat, Good Sirs, as does our own.

She is near Para Creek. Marta, is with her. They are searching inside the edges of the forest wall, looking for unknown genera of blossoms and strange chrysalises, looking and describing and collecting.

Marta walks ahead, hacking with a machete at the dense overgrowth, the frequent surfacing of sawgrass. She points to a branch on a tree. Maria Sybilla approaches, rapid and silent, ah, yes, ja, ja. There is a red caterpillar with yellow stripes crawling along the top of the branch. It is feeding on the leaves that grow there. The movement of Maria Sibylla's hand is sure and quick, scooping the caterpillar from the branch and placing it firmly and unharmed in a jar with a bit of the bark and some leaves from the tree. The caterpillar will be brought back to her study to be kept with the others, the numbers of her specimens growing, in jars with mesh tops, in wire cages, in bottles stoppered with cork.

They turn a corner of the forest into a lush growth of

Rafflesia, the plant is called the corpse plant because it smells like rotting flesh, the flower is enormous, glowing bright orange, the diameter measured in feet, the thick tubular stem. The Indians extract a liquid from the stem that is used to stop the flow of blood. Marta tells her that it is also used to counteract the bites of snakes, that it quickly reverses the effect of the poison in the bloodstream though the flesh has already grown dark. Marta tells her that the seeds of the peacock flower are used to bring about the menses, that the female slaves swallow the seeds to abort their fetuses, to preserve the unborn child from a life of slavery like their own.

Branches bend and scrape in the breeze, airy and delicate, twisting and turning, continually changing direction, and the shrill shrieks of the howler monkeys high above, flying, torsos twisting and turning, arms outstretched, teeth bared, panting and screaming.

The old woman appears as if out of nowhere, she is all bone and sinewy and nerves cells dancing on the coarse, black flesh of her neck and shoulders, and down along her arms, the heavy bracelets on her wrists, the nerve cells dancing into the bones of her fingers. She is speaking in the Creole that the Dutch call Neger-Englen, and Maria Sibylla can understand some of the words: *tree, hanging or suspended?, comb, bird.* And all the time the old woman is speaking, a sack near her feet is screeching and humping. The old woman reaches inside the sack and firmly holding its neck pulls out a brilliantly colored, huge, young macaw. She hands the macaw to Maria Sibylla, who, avoiding its enormous stabbing beak, takes the frantic bird and covers it with a net to calm it. The old woman points to herself and says, *Mama Cato, Mama Cato.* Maria Sibylla repeats the name, *Mama Cato.* The old woman wants to trade for the macaw. She points to the sack filled with supplies that is slung over Maria

Sibylla's shoulder, indicating she wants it emptied on the ground. Maria Sibylla tells Marta to take the sack and empty it on the ground. The old woman points to a bright blue piece of salempouri cloth and a green tree frog in a stoppered jar of liquid. Maria Sibylla nods to indicate that she may take them. The leave-taking is abrupt; the old woman quickly disappears back into the jungle. Marta steps forward and begins putting everything back inside the sack, while Maria Sibylla continues holding the now-silent macaw.

Mosquitoes swarm and puncture her skin.

Beads of blood form on the punctures.

The blood is trickling where the mosquitoes have bitten.

And then another and another puncture in her skin.

Sirs, A most uncommon discovery. A butterfly exactly one half male and the other half female, the rear on one side being male, and on the other female.

In the Kerkstraat Gardens there had been butterflies, benign creatures, but not so beautiful as these. These are more beautiful, but not benign.

Somewhere the ants are taking down a tapir. The pig does not stand a chance. As the ants dig in. As the flesh falls away. As the spirit of the beast rushes out through its head. The slight whoosh of sound each time she pins an insect. Her back stiff and straight. Inside the house, the light glows from the candles.

"I have looked at several cane pieces for farming," Mathew van der Lee announces during the evening meal. "There are some acres south from here, at the mouth of Sara Creek."

"So far to the south, Mr. van der Lee," the Widow Ivenes responds with alarm. "We will never see you if you move so far to the south."

"You will visit often, Widow Ivenes, and spend your time much as you like."

"The Sara Creek region is not thought safe, Mr. van der Lee," says Esther Gabay. "The runaways are settled near to there."

"It is said the numbers of the runaways are few, Madame Gabay."

"The numbers may be few, Mr. van der Lee," says Esther Gabay, "but the assaults on the sugar farms are many."

"And the expeditions of our soldiers most often fail in their efforts to recapture them," adds Doctor Peter Kolb.

"But there are slaves recaptured everyday, Doctor Kolb," says Mathew van der Lee.

"And everyday there are more runaways," counters the Doctor, "and more violence against the plantations."

"The violence is not likely to continue," insists Mathew van der Lee. "How many slaves will risk the punishments if caught?—the beatings, the mutilations. There is one of your colleagues in Paramaribo, Doctor Kolb, whose job it is to amputate limbs from recaptured runaways."

"The punishments do not deter the runaways," says Doctor Peter Kolb. "Their sensibility is not as ours, Mr. van der Lee."

"I am not persuaded of that view," says Mathew van der Lee.

"Nor am I, I would agree, Mr. van der Lee," says the Widow Iveness. And then turning to Maria Sibylla, "What has science to say on the subject?"

"It seems not a matter for science, Dear Widow Ivenes."

"What of your work then?" the Widow persists in drawing Maria Sibylla into the conversation.

"My work progresses, Widow Ivenes."

"And extraordinary work it is, Madame Sibylla," says the Widow.

"What is extraordinary," says Esther Gabay, "is that so much effort should be taken in the interest of insects."

"There is greater fortune to be made in sugar cane," says Doctor Peter Kolb.

"My interest here is not in sugar, Doctor Kolb."

"Madame Sibylla's interest is to witness nature and not to mine for its material potentiality," says Mathew van der Lee, staring openly at Maria Sibylla. "She is an artist and a scientist, Doctor Kolb, and those are the interests which occupy her. Much as my own interest in collecting has occupied me. It is true I now seek fortune here in sugar, but I have not lost interest in the natural world."

"Indeed well spoken," says the Widow Ivenes.

Mr. van der Lee. Come see. He moves closer to her and he sees. It is one of the moth pupae she brought with her on the journey from Amsterdam, so that she might witness the completion of their transformations. There in a cage in the Surimombo study. The moth has broken through its shell, broken out at last from chrysalis, after these months since its ocean crossing. The small, delicate moth clings to the wires of the cage with its wings wildly flapping. It is of the species *Phalaena tau*, its wings appearing moist in the light from the candles, and the flames flare up and cast shadows on the wall. Of the moth. Of the woman. And the man.

The next day she has an accident. She reaches out for a caterpillar on the leaf of a tree in the forest near to the main house. It is a vibrant blue-black, inky and depthless, two ruby stripes along the sides of its body. Sensing her presence, it lifts its head, raises it high as if surveying, then lowers and lifts it again, and then it stops with its body rigid and its head raised. She quickly cups it in her palm and is met with a stinging pain so severe she can barely open her hand to release the caterpillar into the cage. Her body flushes hot. Her hand swells to twice its size and she can hardly remain standing. There is the feeling of sinking, of wanting to let go to the ground and let sleep come, of wanting the floor of the forest—green and lush like the sofas of dowagers, thick and soft in rich velvets and muted shades of olive—to receive her. She sinks down to the bottom of the tree trunk and waits for the dizziness to pass. Almost immediately an apprehension wells up inside her. She feels a sensation on her legs. She pulls the fabric of her clothing up and sees small black wood ticks that despite the layers of her skirt have in seconds covered the flesh of her lower legs and are swarming towards her thighs and her abdomen. She leaps up, surprises a giant macaw on a branch not far above, the bird lifts its wings and shrieks, the shrieks soar up through the branches and the bird follows. She walks as quickly as she can, though she is still unsteady and somewhat dizzy from the poison still in her body. Breathing is difficult. The air is thick with moisture, it is all moisture, the air turned fluid, a substance not breathed but swallowed into the lungs, the chest cavity fills and congests. She is moving forward, returning to the Surimombo main house, in any case she wasn't far, had not gone far. And to the bathing house where she applies an ointment to her legs and her belly following a washing treatment with a brush and harsh liquids. The skin red now, scrubbed raw. Reclaimed. Clean. The bathing house is cool, the water strained through sieves to keep the sand out, the floor polished stone and cool on the bottoms of her feet, and the small black parasitic insects, all to the last one, fallen to the floor, inert, a little pile at her feet, then washed, washed away by the water. She balances herself, holding on with one hand to the wall of the dressing room in the bathing house, the dressing room with its conveniences, small round soaps in smooth clay dishes, jars of salts for soaking, fragrant oils, fresh cut peacock flowers, a bath sheet for drying her body, a white muslin robe for wrapping up in, the bathing house itself shaded by palmetto leaves falling like folds of fabric over the wooden structure. Now a lizard appears on the outside of the window, it is one of the small lizards that are everywhere in Surinam. Its body is pressed against the mesh that serves as a screen, the sun's rays make it glow, crystalline, the body transparent, shot through by the sun so that she can see the insides clear and shining, and the long thin vein that runs from its head down to its tail, and extends out to each of its four legs, and to each of the toes of its webbed feet. Dear lizard, remarkable beast, lit by the afternoon sun, pierced through by a ray of white light, human eyes are blinded by so much light, by so much heat and brightness. She goes over to the window to view the lizard more closely and sees Mathew van der Lee off a ways in the distance; she sees his figure in the white sun, against the bleached out grasses near the sugar fields. He is walking with his hands clasped behind his back. Later, he will ask if he might accompany her again up the coast to the ocean, on one of her hunts there for shells. They will set out as if on a picnic, carrying charcoals and vellums, specimen boxes and killing jars. They will walk over sand strewn with branches and mollusk shells, nests of seaweed, dead fish, ghost crabs heaped together on the shore. She will walk erect with her back straight, with her shoes caked with mud and the bottom of her dress wet and dragging. Mathew van der Lee will make a light-hearted comment about the mud on her shoes, and just as he does his own feet will sink some inches into the ground. He will reach out as if to touch her when she looks down at his feet, but then will quickly withdraw his arm.

And a running off of water in the bath house, her legs good, her waist narrow, her feet long, slender, somewhat bony, a running off of water, scented powders, the tortoise comb, her hair undone and hanging down below her shoulders in dark wet pieces, like a witch she thinks, die Hexe, bezaubernde Frau.

She descends the staircase from her second floor suite of the Surimombo main house, the interior copied faithfully in the style of her adopted city of Amsterdam, her city of Amsterdam with its cold nights, and with its gabled, corniced structures, and with its canals with their bodies of dead waters. And the German township where she was born—Frankfort am Mein—where she spent all her early life and formed her identity, is distant now, and she will never return there again, and will have no cause or wish to return. She is pale and fatigued, and the last of the light is fading; night is falling and a blanket of blackness will soon cover the house while the lodgers are gathered for the evening meal. The candles in the dining room will draw to the window pale moths, as pale as she is, unable to resist the fiery center, and their wings will beat against the glass, pounding and bruising their plump bodies; they will look like ghosts in the dark, eager and hungry, seeking their shadow selves there in the flame. And all the while the other moths, the specimens she has collected, will remain safe in their cages, quiet in the darkened room. And when the night has fully fallen, the lantern flies will come out with their lights glittering.

She lifts her hand to the back of her neck to wipe the beads of perspiration away. She drinks boiled water left to cool, dips her fingers into the water and touches her brow, her neck. The heat is draining her of blood and spirit, sucking the marrow out from her bones and leaving them to ache at night, her arms and her legs ache each night and she is restless on the bed. She finds it difficult to sleep from the aching and the restlessness.

She descends the stairs now down to supper, to where the others are already seated in the dining room.

"You are pale, Madame Sibylla. Are you unwell?"

"It is nothing, Dr. Kolb. It is only the heat. No. Nothing. Or if anything, the heat."

"Yes the heat. How is your work progressing?"

"Well."

"And your hand? Has it healed from the accident?"

"Yes."

"I am a physician, Madame Sibylla. Will you permit me to have a look at it? You would not want it to fester."

"It is nothing Doctor. Kolb. It was only a reaction to the pathetic creature's venom. As you see, it has completely subsided."

Drums are beating. Drums are beating in the night. The sound of the drums comes from the forest beyond Piki Ston where the runaways have erected their settlements. The drums cannot come from the plantations; on the plantations the black slaves are forbidden to drum, forbidden to send their rebel messages. She has seen what happens to those who disobey. She has seen the bloody stump where a hand once was, and the body flogged skinless, and a raw, pulpy mass where the flesh once was, and the body kept alive in ruin.

She is fatigued. It can be seen on her face, and in the way she comports herself, in the way her breath comes labored, and her eyes appear clouded and distant.

It is the heat. And the poison still in her body from the caterpillar's sting. Night has fallen and the window is covered with moths that are drunk on the light from the flames of the candle. The moths will die, just as she believes that she will die, that the heat of the sun will kill her, that the harshness of this place will end her life. She is still weak, and still vertiginous from the caterpillar's venom.

The venom in her body has increased her fatigue, and her nights are beset by dreams, and by visions that appear and disappear, alternately beautiful and terrifying.

In a dream she is menaced by an animal, it comes around in front of her, an aggressive look in its eyes,

She is standing listening to the river, the still, glassy surface shining in the sun, the sun's rays rippling on the surface, she is standing looking out to the bend in the river, a distance farther and white waters start to form, the current goes crazy with white waters, a little while more and rapids, a little while more and the water gushing and pounding, crazy water, a little while more and crazy water, dashing against rocks, the falls to take you to the bottom, and the devil's egg, the rock that is perched above the water, the dashing crazy water, the falls are Piki Ston Falls, along the river bank the monkeys with their perpetual screaming, is it with warning? is it with ill intent? the violent screams of the monkeys, but here where she is standing the river is still, there is no ripple, the sun shines in streaks on the placid surface.

Small, sweeter than the alligator pear, the sweet red fruit of the yucca.

The butterflies are made of feathers. She points to all the tiny little feathers.

In her drawings the themes come slowly into focus, a merest outline, a shadowy creature, and then she adds light.

The theme of primulas with nun moth, plum branch and pale tussock, cotton leaf jatropha, mimicry moth, antaeus moth.

The theme of the lantern fly, meadow larkspur and pease blossom moth, various beetles and a harlequin beetle.

The theme of four dead finches. The birds are pathetic the way she portrays them. There is no question they are dead, quintessentially and permanently dead. Flight no more. For the small brown birds.

And the sun breaking through enormous,

it sears the flesh, the ground, the wooden frame of the Surimombo main house.

In a clearing in the forest Marta has wrapped herself in salempouri cloth, and the bright blue of the fabric is shining, and she is dancing, she is spinning in front of Maria Sibylla. The dance can stop the fierce thunderstorms and the torrents of the rains, and Marta is dancing to bring an end to the rains.

But the sky is gray, and the heavy rains are again threatening.

There is a crocodile somewhere in the meh-nu bushes with its jaws snapping. There is the sound the leaves make when the wind blows through them. A storm rising up. The scream of the toucani. In the Surimombo Jungle there had been a trail of dead toucani. Or had they fallen randomly? And the crocodile is creeping out from the swamp onto the jungle floor. And the rain will cause a lake to form in the jungle.

The leaves of the Ku-deh-deh fortify the heart. Marta holds the fingers of her right hand outstretched above her heart, her eyes are dark and excited as she picks the waxy leaves and crushes them

And all the while Maria Sibylla is searching among the vines and the creepers.

But what about the moth, the newly hatched *Phalaena tau?* Ah, the *Phalaena tau* has been recently transformed. Has broken through its shell and been released. It was Maria Sibylla herself who released the moth. Into the heat. Into the harshness and the freedom of the jungle.

The *Phalaena tau* has flown to make her own way in the jungle.

And Maria Sibylla is searching for the new moth, the stranger.

Among the vines, the creepers, the rosettes of leaves, the night-smelling orchids, the mora excelsa.

Along the branches of the unnamed tree.

The blossoms are red and the tree is unnamed. And the roots of the tree are buried. In the jungle earth that turns to water. The ground is soft, the leaves are shimmering.

And she is silent now and waiting. The voluptuousness of the time of waiting.

She has been walking for so long her feet are burning, but her eyes are searching everywhere. For you, the stranger, the promise of what she has come for.

She is looking for you, bewitched by you.

In the green, indistinct light of the jungle. That filters down through the branches of the trees.

The screaming birds, their calls harsh, piercing.

The jungle orchids, the delicate tree orchid, the air-borne orchid with its tentacles dangling, and covered in small white flowers, its musky scent, its mouth that never opens.

She is breathless and her heart is beating rapidly.

The heat pours down but she no longer notices, she is intent on finding you.

You are her loadstone, her wish, her temptation, her consummation.

Entranced she is looking, in a fever she is looking.

For the slanted traces that will lead her to you.

The small paroxysms, the silent heartbeat, the throbbing.

But where is it that Maria Sibylla finds you? So quiet. On the branch of the unknown tree? It is a secret tree, so secret even the Amerindians do not know its name, the Tree of Paradise? The tree of the fall from grace? The tree the serpent wrapped itself around and whispered, offering its fruit, and the leaves stinging like nettles, and you clinging with your tiny feet, having taken hold to suck the sweetness, the snake there with you all the time, all wound around its branches, and you as you had always been, from that first hour when you were the first one, the first to take hold upon that branch, to nourish on that unknown, unnamed genus, and having had your fill of eating to spin and spin the silk that would enclose you, and keep you safe inside that first of all enclosures, protected and unharmed, to sleep for the season of your transformation.

II

There is a beast, there is a beast in Surinam. A white beast seen prowling in the grasses near the sugar farms. The Indians say it is the jinn of a demon that lives under Piki Ston Falls. That it will come and slash slash with its teeth as large as Waha leaves. That it will come to take its dwendi, its lady mama girl to make its wild monkey bride, to make its wild monkey bride girl running. It has hair that is white and sticks out like the shoots of white copal; it has hands that are claws and it stands on its legs like a man.

The beast stalks the sugar farms while the day steams with heat, or, at night stalks the shanties of the slaves.

It is the slaves who see the beast, but sometimes it is one of the Europeans. Like the white overseer at Plantation Davilaar. The man was relieving himself near the edges of the sugar field when he saw an animal crouched a distance from him. The beast reared up and the man turned on his heels and ran.

"It is only an hysteria of the Africans and the Indians," Esther Gabay tells the others over morning meal.

The serving girl brings trays to the table, sets out platters of ham, baskets heaped high with breads, eggs, cassava cakes, green tea, coffee, chocolate.

"It is only an hysteria," Esther Gabay repeats, "or a fabrication that has been hatched by the runaways."

"Hatched to what purpose, Madame Gabay?" asks Doctor Peter Kolb.

"To stir unrest among the slaves, Doctor Kolb."

"It is more likely a wolf, Madame Gabay," says the Doctor. "It would not be the first time that a lone wolf, displaced from the pack, or with its instincts otherwise upset, has been known to attack at humans."

"There are no wolves here, Doctor Kolb."

"It is a species capable of turning up, Madame Gabay, of one day making an appearance. There are many forces that will drive a pack, or that will provoke a lone wolf to wander into a new territory."

"I have lived here all my life, Dr. Kolb, and have never heard rumor of wolves."

"They have been known to turn up, Madame Gabay."

"We have never had wolves, Doctor Kolb."

"We may have one now, Madame Gabay."

"What is your opinion?" the Widow Ivenes asks turning suddenly to Maria Sibylla. "Do you believe it is an hysteria?"

"I believe we should not waste our days with speculation on a creature that may or may not exist. I, in any case, shall not waste my days on it. We must trust in the will of the Divine Being, Widow

Ivenes, and in our Fate, and I in my work that it is necessary I continue."

"Will you continue in the forests?" asks Doctor Peter Kolb.

"I shall continue as I must, Doctor Kolb."

"Would it not be wise, Madame Sibylla, to avoid the forests?" asks Mathew van der Lee.

"Would you dissuade me, Mr. van der Lee?"

"For your safety it would be cautious, Madame Sibylla."

"For my safety, Mr. van der Lee, I should never have left Frankfurt am Main for Amsterdam, and later Amsterdam for Friesland, or Friesland for Amsterdam once again, and now made this journey to Surinam. Safe, inside my house, Mr. van der Lee, might I still not fall ill and languish and die?"

She prepares after morning meal to travel with Marta into the forest right outside of Paramaribo. The other slaves have pleaded not to have to accompany them, apprehensive as they are now of the beast.

Marta, who has begun to copy the makeshift style of Maria Sibylla, wears an overall that she has sewn, and under it a shirt Esther Gabay has given her left behind by a previous lodger. Both women wear hats. Their feet and their legs are well covered.

Marta is perspiring, the perspiration runs in large beads from beneath the brim of her hat and down her face, down her Indian nose with the hint of a bump in it, her nostrils flare, her lower lip protrudes.

Maria Sibylla brings her hand behind her own neck, and reaches down along the back of her left shoulder, she digs her fingers into her flesh, a relaxation from the heat, an easement from the weight of the vellum, the charcoal, the brushes, the nets and the killing jars.

The women are in a small patch of clearing where the light shines down unfiltered and blinding. They raise their hands above their eyes to see.

Hummingbirds in crimson. In vibrant purples and greens. In vests of metallic colors that gleam and change as the light hits them, or as the birds shift the positions of their bodies. The birds are barely larger than the butterflies. Hovering above the branches and singing in unison. There are some sixty of them at least, and they are singing a mating song. Small and glittering like precious stones. All hovering and in song. Maria Sibylla surmises they are males, it is the striking colors that tell her, the males wardrobed for mating and singing in chorus. The voices are not beautiful—their song does not have the sweetness of the helabeh, nor the lyric quality of the thrush. They make a rasping sound, a thin, high pitched tone such as stone scraping metal.

The birds come into focus like the details on the canvases of certain paintings, at first mere abstract shape and color, and then gradually sharpening, becoming discernable.

A little deeper into the forest and again they see hummingbirds, but these, though alive, are not singing.

They are caught in the traps that the shamans have set for them, their bright metallic colors gleaming in the nets in the sun, but their bodies are limp now, no longer hovering, the birds are caught in the shamans' nets, the blur of wingbeat has stopped and they are trapped, forty or fifty at least, perhaps more in the nets of the shamans.

The shamans have set traps for the hummingbirds. That is their diet Marta tells Maria Sibylla—to be fed exclusively on the flesh of hummingbirds.

And the mating song is deadly for the hummingbirds, to be caught in the nets of the shamans.

The sugar farms veer off in all directions: Machado; Castillo; Alvamant; Cordova; Davilaar; Boavista; Providentia. The plantations with their yearly harvests. With the intense heat of their boiling houses and the slitting of the cane to test for sweetness. And the sugar that is dripping from the stalks. It is the wedding at the Castillo Plantation and it has brought all of the township of Surinam out for the celebration. The bride is the daughter of Castillo and the groom is the elder Alvamant. She is seventeen, while the elder Alvamant is forty-three and twice a widower. The bride is virginal and sweet like the sugar cane.

It is from the Castillo wedding that the famous portrait of the men derives: twenty-two of them in all, posed like the Officers of the Militia at one of the banquet tables. Doctor Peter Kolb is in the portrait, seated looking towards the left, and gesturing with his hands in conversation. Mathew van der Lee is also shown in the portrait, his expression animated and turned in semi-profile facing Doctor Peter Kolb. The eyes of the other men stare straight ahead, the groom at center expectant and flushed.

From this wedding, too, comes the portrait of Maria Sibylla dressed in garden silk and satin capuchin. Her mood is high and her skin glows in the heat. She is fresh from one of the wedding dances, it was a cotillion and this done in turns, each with a different partner. She has had several of these turns with Mathew van der Lee.

The Widow Ivenes tells the wedding party her dream of the white beast. In the dream the Widow is a child again. She is leading the beast on a chain and the animal is following docile and quiet, trotting like a little dog behind the Child Ivenes. But then a wind starts up and the fur of the white beast begins to ripple like a lion's mane, and the Child Ivenes and the beast move steadily against the wind, and the beast lets out a ferocious roar and throws its head back, all the while roaring, and the Child Ivenes' hair blows free from her cap.

But the beast is not a dream at the Providentia Plantation. A female slave has been mauled and her infant snatched from her. The woman had given birth the night before, and in the morning fell behind the others at the edges of the sugar fields. The beast appeared out of nowhere and sprang at the woman and tore at her flesh, and the woman dropped her baby to the ground. When she did, the beast stopped its attack and let go of the woman, then grabbed the baby from the ground and ran into the jungle.

The black men are crouched outside the flap door of one of the shanties.

Jama-Santi, the child who was witness to the attack, is brought by the men to tell what he saw. He was in the bushes at the edge of the sugar field where he saw the woman resting with her infant. He saw the beast nearby as if in hiding. The beast came across the field on all four paws, like this, and Jama-Santi moves forward in a crouch to show the men, and then it slashed at the woman, rising up on its two legs until it was taller than a man, and then it knocked the woman to the ground and ran off with her infant.

crocodile man, monkey man, alligator man.

There is a bristling on the backs of the black men's necks; it goes unnoticed for the moment by the Dutch. There are the words that are repeated in the shanties, by the African slaves speaking in their Neger-Englen.

alligator man, mystery man, crocodile man.

But what more is to be said about the wedding party, about the feasting and the dance, the endless rounds of the cotillions? Or for that matter what more is to be said about the wedding couple? The chaste bride. The expectant groom. Shall we call attention to them now and to the coming of the night with its sweet outpouring like the liquid from the sugar cane? The stalk is slit deep, and the syrup of the sugar is dripping.

Maria Sibylla has gone out behind the main house of the Castillo Plantation and has been followed by Mathew van der Lee. "Mr. van der Lee," she says when she sees him, "Here, come." Her black hair is piled high upon her head, and her shoulders are bare, and she is thin in her garden silk. "Madame Sibylla," says Mathew van der Lee as he approaches her.

They will be returning soon to Surimombo.

It is early evening, just before the nightfall. The day's work is over on the sugar farms. The slaves talk about the beast; they say its eyes are malignant, flashing. And the land moves out from the sea down into the jungle.

It is her desire that is driving her to seek beyond the limits that would otherwise constrain her. In the morning she goes out alone into the fields, behind the house, into the small forest, alone into the jungle

From a distance she thinks they are large birds, but as she approaches she sees they are monkeys. There is a brood of them on the ground in the clearing. The monkeys are curious, especially the youngest ones, they approach without fear to smell her out. A baby grabs at the bottom of her overall. But when she steps forward the baby lets go and runs back to the rest. The adults approach menacing, their shrieks deafening, then all at once they pull themselves into the trees.

When the monkeys clear, Maria Sibylla sees the old black woman, Mama Cato. She has brought cowrie shells and beetles to trade for fabric and a sheet of vellum. Mama Cato is running back and forth in front of Maria Sibylla, shouting something that the Dutch woman does not understand. Then Mama Cato stops her shouting and her running and throws her head back and makes a call like a bird. Her call brings toucans. The toucans are flying all around her, the toucons in flight, flapping their wings above Mama Cato.

When the trading is finished, the old woman moves back into the jungle and the toucans disappear above the trees.

But something else is moving now, a hint of something moving among the trees.

Or is it only the way the land moves out from the sea into the jungle. And the swaying of the branches in the trees.

Are there footsteps? Footfall? When Mama Cato has left her alone in the forest? The sound of thrashing against the jungle growth.

Is it the beast? The white beast stalking? On its diurnal ritual? The heaving and sighing of the beast.

And in the distance the cracking of the whips back on the sugar farms.

That evening at supper the five of them gather. How familiar now the sight of them gathered. The plates are passed from left to right, the way they have always been passed since the first evening of her arrival. And the lodgers are seated where they have always been seated since the moment they first sat down. The talk tonight is of the beast, of the incident at Providentia Plantation. Since the attack on the female slave there has been talk of little else at Surimombo. And Esther Gabay, for all her fears of its effect to stir unrest among the slaves, is unable to control the conversation, to stop the steady stream of discourse on the beast.

"What is called a beast is sometimes merely a deformity," says Doctor Peter Kolb, "such as the deformity of the mystery people, the Ewaipanoma, who are born without a head."

"But the Ewaipanoma are not a real people," says Esther Gabay.

The moths have come and are beating at the window, attracted by the glow of the candles in the dining room, and the window is covered with moths, just as each night since her arrival the window has been covered with moths, and it is as though nature has conspired with its own ritual, and the window is all movement and pulsation. But look who has come this night to take advantage. It is the spider called a wolf spider because it preys in the manner of wolves. It has come to hunt on the window on which the moths have lighted with such compulsion that even when the spider makes its presence known, the moths are unable to flee. For the moths are transfixed there by the light from the candles, bearded, with their bodies flattened, pressed close to the window. And the window provides a feast this night for the spider.

Or later in the salon, or in her laboratory, or in the bedroom of her suite of rooms where the cocoon of the mosquito netting hangs all around her, and the fabric of the netting is soft and silky to the touch.

Despite the layers of the netting, the mosquitoes puncture her flesh, as they have done many times since her arrival.

But who comes dancing in these hours before she sleeps. Gaunt. Thin. He is thin. Like an insect. Imagine.

Dancing in the hours before she sleeps.

If the beast has sport with you, you die, if the beast touches your mama woman you have babies that come out with heads like crocodiles, if the beast touches you, you feel red pain rising in your loins. That is what the Indians say. And that is what the Africans also say. The Indians and Africans are of one mind about the beast. It is only the Dutch who say something different.

The beast is not a joke. The beast kills you. Do you know the beast? Is the beast the Ewaipanoma without a head? How can they live without a head? How can they eat you without a head? It is a mystery. It is a question that does not have an answer. The

Ewaipanoma live in the deep jungle. But no one can live in the deep jungle. Only the Ewaipanoma and the Africans and the Indians when they are running. They are like dogs when they are running and they are trying to flee their masters. They are running from the slashing of the whip. The women running too. The women running from the whip. And from the use that is made of them. As many times as is desired. Though not desired by them. And they are like wild dogs the women when they are running into the deep jungle, where the Dutch man tries to follow but gets eaten by the crocodile. But if he finds the dog, oh, no, oh no. If he finds the dog. In the jungle.

The beast has struck and infected with fear the imaginations of the captive peoples, the Amerindians with their russet faces, proud under the whip, and the Africans, too, also proud, and watchful.

The white men beat the slaves with whips, they do not care that they are descended from the tribal princes.

The sudden raids and the enslavements. The spirit cast down a thousand times, a thousand times and gnashings . . . bitter bitter.

But what is the beast? Is it the jinn of a demon hiding under Piki Ston Falls? The falls are high and the water rushes.

Where did the beast come from, appearing out of nowhere? How can the beast appear out of nowhere? Out of nothing? It must come from somewhere.

Here is a white beast: On the Cordova Plantation, Jacob Cordova is punishing a black man for drumming.

But in the deep jungle, past the Nickerie, along the Saramacca River, past the swamp lands with its crocodiles, in the deep jungle that is thick with the liana, there are the settlements of the runaways, there are the fire hearths going and the women cooking at the fire hearths outside the new shanties, and the Dutch man cannot follow here, cannot get past the crocodile and the liana, and the black man is drumming and drumming and drumming.

She is infected now with malaria.

The malaria has her and her eyes are bleary, boiling, the heat has worn her down and the mosquito has overcome her, and she is hollow, her bones are hollow, and her skin has become rough and parched, and hot to the touch, and glistening in the darkened room. Esther Gabay has ordered the thick dark curtains pulled across the window to keep out the light from the sun. And in the dark it is as though Maria Sibylla is glowing, as though her skin is glowing. Her lips have swollen and are thick now, and dry, and her tongue, too, has swollen, and is thick inside her mouth, and her speech is slurred in her delirium, and her words come out in fragments and make no sense. She is saying something about a tulip in the Netherlands, or two river pigs, approaching, and sinking down into silence.

where are you, Maria Sibylla? Mari? Mari? in a thick Dutch accent.

she has a heaviness in her legs, the slowing down of her pulse, the heaviness climbing in her legs.

she cannot breathe, the heaviness has made her breathless.

the fever has made her pale, drawn, brought a dryness to her lips, as if parched, faded, and the air filled up with water draws her body fluids like a sponge, in drops it draws her body fluids from her.

she is in a place that is uninhabitable, it is filled with a substance that she knows cannot sustain her.

there is a tree sloth in her path. hanging limp and in unimaginable pleasure in the shade of a Mora tree.

and her heart beating, hard

and her breath shallow

she is on the Cerro de la Compana, the mountain that is called Bell Mountain located south of the Savannah in Surinam.

white stones rise up on the mountain, the boulders rise white and can be seen from all directions, rising up on the mountain, where there are no trees, only the boulders that rise up to the peaks.

or she is in her father's study looking at the drawing table, at the scene for a still life set on the drawing table.

it is the book of flowers open

the book of insects dreaming

Maria. Maria Sibylla.

and she is sinking down, inside her fever, and sinking down, and down inside her dreams.

Surimombo with its rolling fields of sugar cane, the way the stalk breaks.

and the pale emptying of the darkness.

she is inside the netting, the mosquito netting that is brushing against her like cobwebs, when she tries to move, when she tries to lift up, when she raises her arm, or turns from her back to her side.

or she is walking with Mathew van der Lee along the seashore.

it is his specialty, he tells her, the shore of the sea.

he is speaking and his breath is continuous, it is the absence of pauses that allows his breath to be continuous.

the African slaves hiding in the old abandoned gardens.

amidst the screaming birds, the macaws that scream loudest, the howler monkeys that roar like the jaguars.

her eyes are black with the dilation of her pupils, the bites have punctured her, have left deposits deep inside her, the seeds of the malaria have been planted inside her, and have left her forever assailable.

and Doctor Peter Kolb with his bag of tricks coming in and out of her room, looking now stern, now grave, now perplexed, now fatigued and hopeless, resigned as though he has exhausted all that he can offer, with his bag, with his hands, with his hands thick and sometimes shaking, and yet the shaking is ignored as he, Doctor Kolb, puts his hands first on her head, and then at the base of her throat, and on her neck and on her shoulders, listening, to her breathing, listening to her labored breathing.

and Mathew van der Lee inquiring of Doctor Kolb, often several times in a single day inquiring, asking after the progress of Maria Sibylla, of her recovery, his own face blanched and creased with his concern, or sometimes waiting outside her suite of rooms for the Doctor to exit, or at cards in the evening distracted.

but Marta, too, has been coming into the sick woman's room, at night when the doctor has left, and Esther Gabay is aware of it and does not approve, but does not stop it. Marta brings liquids to drink and some to apply as a compress, and some that have been ground into a paste, or infused in a glass, and in the end these prove the cure.

In the end these prove the cure,

and the world again becomes visible,

and the sun breaks through again completely, to sear the flesh, the ground, the wooden frame of the main house at Surimombo.

As soon as she is able, Maria Sibylla sets out with Marta, they go no farther than the small forest behind the Surimombo sugar fields, the forest is lush with peacock flowers.

INSECT DREAMS 47

Her eyes still ringed with the tiredness left by the malaria, she wears no hat, her hair falls past her shoulders.

The world again surrounds her,

the calls of birds, the hum of insects,

on the branches of the trees caterpillars.

The world again surrounds her and she is working in the forest,

the sweep of her net across the jungle floor,

but while she is working, the slaves are hiding.

The slaves are hiding, wearing hats with gold trim; with iron pots and bolts of cloth, with cowrie shells, sweet oil, candles, pigs, sheep, combs.

And the beast has come sniffing across the sugar fields, and the children hiding in the bushes, or in their hammocks, or in their cribs in the shanties that cannot hold them, and their mothers are saying, oh no, oh no.

The beast has come trotting with the legs of his trousers flapping.

It is on the Machado plantation. Where the beast is reflected in the eyes of the child Josie. The beast is reflected in the eyes, in the eyes of the black child Josie who has just been purchased by Jorge Machado.

The girl is twelve and already has her menses, she is twelve and thin and delicate with dark eyes and long legs.

It is on the Machado plantation, and involves Jorge Machado himself, the look of shock in Josie's eyes, the look of fear, of terror, and then of shame, and the touch of the man who has grabbed her, the man who owns her, the man whose property she is.

The weight of Jorge Machado's neck is pressed against the child Josie's face, and his arms have pinned her arms to their sides, and what he is doing to her, she cannot stop him, his thick neck that is pressed against her mouth, his shoulder that is digging into her breast, his flesh that is pushed into hers, and what he is doing to her,

and her eyes are open and staring.

Where is the mama of the child Josie? The mama is so far away now. And the mama cannot protect her. And the daddy cannot protect her. Where is the daddy of the child Josie?

It is from fear, perhaps from fear and anger, perhaps from the aggrievance to her body, or from the weight of his neck against her face, or from his arms which have pinned her, or the pain from what he is doing to her, the child Josie cannot stop herself she bites Jorge Machado. It is on his neck that she bites him, his neck that has been pressed against her mouth, she sinks her teeth deep into his neck, as he penetrates her, and his shock to feel it,

and his fist pounding down on her mouth,

and her teeth that are broken, and the blood filling up in her mouth.

He rears up like a beast and brings Josie up with him, and Josie is screaming, and the blood is pouring out from her mouth.

But that is not enough to contain the rage of Jorge Machado.

He has a rage that cannot be contained and he spills it out on the child Josie.

And her screams pour out with the blood from her mouth.

And Jorge Machado is pounding and pounding, with his fist like a hammer he pounds her, and her arms flail against him, she is trying to protect herself with her flailing arms, with her arms that flail against him,

until he twists both her arms in their sockets,

and her arms are hanging limp from their sockets,

until Jorge Machado fully spends his rage and by the savage force of his own massive arms he tears the arms out from the sockets of the child Josie.

"There is your beast, Madame Gabay," Maria Sibylla says solemnly, having listened with full attention to the account. "And there is your beast, Doctor Kolb, there is the wolf that you suspect with its eyes flashing, and with its teeth that rip and tear and rip and tear, and there is your beast, too, Widow Ivenes, your fine white beast that trots behind you like a dog, and it is sitting right beside the beast of Madame Gabay."

That night she dreams that she is on the ship, The Peace, that it has come to take her home. The ship sets sail and she is returning to her home in the Netherlands. She is standing on the deck as the ship leaves the shore, as it sets sail out to the sea. She is standing on the deck and there is still light from the sun, but the air is cold. And when night comes she is still on the deck and it is now very cold. In her dream she can see the moon at three-quarters, and the planets and the stars, all those miles away from her.

The next day she is alone in the small forest, Marta is not with her. It is called the Surimombo Forest because it extends along the edges of the Surimombo Plantation and can be seen from the sugar fields.

It is the day she discovers the little-bird spider. It is a tarantula, covered with hair, straddling its prey, sucking the blood out from a tiny bird. The bird is on its back only a few inches from the nest, its head hanging limp between a fork in the branch. Maria Sibylla is transferring the scene to vellum, painstaking and accurate in her rendering.

She has announced that morning during breakfast she will cut short her visit. On its approaching journey back she will again board The Peace.

It is the heat that is driving her, she has told them, that is prompting her to cut short her visit, and she is still fatigued from her illness, from the malaria, and she believes that if she remains she will not survive, and all the while the heat is breathing itself into her, needling and insistent like the mouth of an insect.

Footsteps approach, she is vaguely aware, the sound of someone thrashing against the jungle growth, she stops drawing and turns in the direction of the footsteps.

It is Mathew van der Lee who has followed her, who has come to seek her out where she is working.

She stands silent, the sun's rays on her.

You are working.
I am working.
Is it true what you said, you will leave soon?
Yes, true, it is true.
But I thought that you might stay.
I am sorry, I must leave, Mr. van der Lee.
Will you not change your mind?
It is too hot, Mr. van der Lee.
I have purchased some cane fields, Madame Sibylla.
You will soon be rich, Mr. van der Lee.

There is something in the shape of his face, its triangularity, and the impression that it gives, there is something in the expression on his face.

And her face still flushed from the malaria.

It will be difficult to leave you, Mr. van der Lee.

He is thin and his lower jaw protrudes slightly. He has the look of a student long past his student days, he is reserved and yet he is intense, he is somewhat delicate and yet there is a strength to him.

And the heat from the sun beating down.

What is the contradiction welling inside her, the contradiction rising inside her? The heat on the one hand—the insidious armies of ants, the wood ticks that in seconds can cover the entirety of the body,

and on the other, everything is lush, lush, and the clouds tinged pink, and the floor of the jungle is thick and soft, so soft you can sink down into it.

Her hair shines black.

Her black hair falling past her shoulders.

Her beating heart, her breathlessness.

And Mathew van der Lee standing before her.

Maria Sibylla stares, then she beckons him closer, motions him to come closer, closer, quiet, puts her fingers to her lips, quiet, quiet, here, come, Mr. van der Lee, and she shows him what it is that she is drawing, the tiny bird that has been vanquished by the spider, the tameless spider still in the act of ravaging the bird, she shows him first on her drawing on the vellum, and then points to the live model on the tree, and they are standing very close now, with their faces nearly touching, and there is the mingling of their breaths in the hot, humid air of the forest, under the branches of the tree, this tree that rises up like an altar, like an altar to which they have brought their supplication, their devotions and their dalliance, their yearning and their desire, and the parrots on the branches high above are screaming, as though the birds are giving voice to the intensity of the drama that is taking place below, to the triumph of the silent spider, and to the agony of the vanquished bird, and to the intentness of the woman and the man, and Maria Sibylla is solemn now, as still as stone, her chest no longer rising and falling with the inhalations and exhalations of her breath, she is no longer breathing, her breath held, held for an impossibly long time, and Mathew van der Lee is so close to her now, and quiet, and he is also barely breathing, his breath also held, until at last in one continuous breath he whispers the words, I thought that I might—I thought that we might, and then Mathew van der Lee goes down on his knees before her.

III

On the deck of the ship there are three figures: Maria Sibylla Merian in ship-dress, a muslin jacket and a chip hat, her body rigid, her face pale; and next to her, her Indianen, Marta, who is dressed much the same as Maria Sibylla, and who is going home with her now to the Netherlands; and on Marta's shoulder a macaw perched with its huge wings that are from time to time flapping; it is the same macaw that had been traded with Mama Cato. The bird has a gold chain fastened to its leg and that in turn is fastened to a heavy bracelet on Marta's wrist, and the bird's feathers are a brilliant mix of yellow and green and turquoise, the yellow is sunflower yellow, like the king's yellow, like Indian dyes and canaries, and the green and the blue are like emerald and cobalt, or a green like mittler's green, or a blue like indigo, steel blue, sapphire.

IV

To Mr. Mathew van der Lee from Maria Sibylla Merian
Surinam, October 5th, 1701
van der Lee Plantation
Paramaribo

Monsieur!
I have received the gentleman's (your) letter of March 19th and read therein that you are surprised to have received no letters from me.
I have also received your previous letters, as well as animals from you on two occasions. The first time they were brought by the apothecary, Mister Jonathaan Petiver, but because I was not in need of such creatures I gave them back to him and thanked

him, requesting that he write to you, telling you I have no use for such animals and did not know what to do with them. For the kind of animals I am looking for are quite different. I am in search of no other animals, but only wish to study certain transformations, how one emerges from the other. Therefore, I would ask you not to send me any more animals, for I have no use for them.

I continue my work and am still doing it, bringing everything to parchment in its full perfection. But everything I did not bring, or did not find at the time when I cut short my journey, cannot now, after so long a period, be similarly rendered, or remembered, or imagined. And there are so many wondrous, rare things that have never come to light before, and which I will now not be able to bring to light. For the heat in your country is staggering, and many were surprised that I survived, and I have still not fully recovered from my malaria. Thus all my memory associated with that time—which even then had the quality of a dream—has become now all the more ephemeral in its proclivity to fade. And that is so much so that what I have preserved on parchment remains as the only tangible reality that I can summon of that time.

On the journey back, Mr. van der Lee, the sky raged for one entire week with storm, and I believed that God had set upon me, that he was pursuing me in the violent wake of the ship, and we all held fast upon the vessel as our only hope for life while day and night the storm raged, and the good captain, sallow, soaked and freezing, did not let go his place at the helm beside the helmsman. Though this I knew only afterwards, as you might guess, for during the storm I was confined to my own quarters, where, never previously sick from motion, I was at that time quite ill. For my weakness from the malaria was still inside me, and that, along with the tossing of the ship brought back my fever, and in my fever I believed, Mr. van der Lee, that I was beset upon by God, so filled as I was with remorse for all that had happened and perhaps as much so for what could not.

It has been my pride for all my life to rely upon my good sense, and to engage the pragmatic view to carry me, and science to inform me, and God to guide and to protect me. But during those days and nights of storm at sea these went out of balance, Mr. van der Lee, and I came to believe that God was in pursuit of me for my weakness, and that the storm had been sent by His intention to fell me, and that the ship would be destroyed and everyone on board along with myself would perish, unfortunate as they had been to journey with me. I came to believe, too, that the sailors had been correct in their judgment of me as a witch. And I counted myself fortunate that the trials for witchcraft had been long since discontinued in the Netherlands, and that the last of these trials (it afterwards being deemed unlawful) had preceded me by a full ninety years. For were that not the case, I was convinced that I would surely be among those numbers of unfortunate women who were hung or burned or drowned. That is how distraught my mind was, Mr.

van der Lee, from the fever and the storm. But then the storm cleared and the ship proceeded forward on a sea that was again calm, and we on board all settled back into its more gentle motion and continued that way for the remainder of the journey.

With that my mind, and my heart, too, became restored, and my days were spent again on deck, where I imagined I could catch the fading scent of the flamboyant trees, and all the other sweet smells of Paramaribo. Marta, whom I brought back from your land to the Netherlands, and released from her condition of servitude, continued to nurture me throughout the journey with infusions of plants. These skills she had learned from her mother, who in turn had learned them from a Shaman in her former village of Kwamalasamoetoe, which in our language means the Bamboo Sand.

It is true I feel a longing for your land. In my ears there is still the sound of the rivers with their surface waters one minute placid, the next roiling. And my thoughts in some strange way are still carried forward by the sweep of those rivers.

There is great beauty in your land, I have never denied it, Mr. van der Lee; there is great beauty along side the brutal harshness. I saw many things and many forms of life that I would elsewise not have seen, and I know you glimpsed and understood them, too. Your land has a multitude of small insects that are rare, and other creatures, fierce and strange and beautiful. I observed the habits formed by these creatures, and observed the way they have their own laws and their own proceedings.

I saw the swarm of ants devouring the spider, and the spider devouring the hummingbird. The Palisade Tree that is called the Tree of Paradise, the apple of Sodom that is red and poisonous, the thickness of the jungle with its tangle of vines, the rats, the storks, the armadillos and the lizards, the toucans and the parrots—all of these have I seen Mr. van der Lee, and they have moved me. I felt, too, the heat that daily burned there, the heat that in the end I believe almost killed me. For the sun burns hotter there than a furnace, and hotter too than the strong clear fires used for boiling the sugar cane. But enough has been spoken of that heat.

It is that other heat I wish to speak of now, a heat capable of arousing in some unwilled and wild way. For it was that heat, too, that breathed itself into me, Mr. van der Lee. And perhaps you will now understand that you wish to recall to me what I have not forgotten.

"What is it you see? What do you see, Madame Sibylla?" How frequently you plied me with such questions, Mr. van der Lee. "What has taken you so far from your home?" you asked. "What keeps you as far? What do you yearn for to the point of dying?"

On that afternoon, Mr. van der Lee, when you followed me into the small forest, the one called Surimombo Forest, you plied me again with these same questions. And with other questions, too, while all the while the heat from the sun was burning me and the moisture in the jungle air was suffocating me. You wore a charm around your neck—untypical of the fastidiousness of your attire—it was a piece of bone, yellowish and slightly curved. You were telling me about the Cerro de la Compana, the mountain that sings like a bell, telling me that it was located south of the savannah on the rolling sandstone hills, and that we must journey there together to hear its bell sound. And I was in the Surimombo Forest and you had followed me and Marta was not with me and I told you again I had already made up my mind to cut short my journey and you went down on your knees before me, down to the leaves on their tiny stems shimmering blue-green on the jungle floor. And the perfume was overpowering from the delicate begonias, the caladiums, the fragile calla lilies, the red passion flowers. And you pushed in against the forest growth, Mr. van der Lee, no longer plying me with questions then, but saying to me instead, "I thought that you might—I thought that we might," and taking me down to the jungle floor with you.

But I must ask you now, as it seems to me I asked you then, there in that staggering heat—what is it that is expected? What can be hoped for now? when it could not be hoped for then?

I could not stay then, Mr. van der Lee, because the heat would have killed me, and apart from that your life on a sugar farm could not be my life. That has not changed. The entrancement that we shared could not endure. There can be room in my life for only one thing, Mr. van der Lee, for only one thing that is passionate and irresistible. The rapture that I seek is in the transformations that I study, and in bringing everything to parchment in its full perfection.

A light rain is falling now with the sun still shining. We call that *Leichter Machen,* or the *Lightening.* It is regarded as bewitching light, Mr. van der Lee, and sometimes it is called the love light or the lovers' light, or interchangeably the festival light. And if you stand at some strategic point you can see this light reflected on the waters of the canals still rippling with the falling rain, and to the eye it looks like countless lights reflected on the waters of the canals, and with the outlines of the bridges on each one. It is a fairy scene, Mr. van der Lee.

But when the rain stops, the strange light will disappear, and all will be as normal again, and no one will know what had been seen. There are visions like that Mr. van der Lee.

I did not answer your earlier letters because there seemed no more on my part to be said, and because I did not wish to give the impression that there was something to be hoped for or expected. I still do not wish to give that impression, Mr. van der Lee.

I write and ask you now to not send animals. For I have no use for them. That is, for the animals such as you sent previously. I wish only to study certain transformations, how one emerges from the other. And I therefore ask you not to send me animals, for I have no use for them.

But if you must send something Mr. van der Lee, send butterflies, small caligo butterflies, diurnal butterflies and ricinis, sactails, jatrophas, moon moths, peacock moths, send primulas with nun moths, pale tussocks and pease blossom moths, tachinid flies and calicoid flies, owl moths and harlequin beetles, or send lantern flies, Mr. van der Lee, in a box that is filled up with the lantern flies, and make certain they are alive when you send them and can be kept living, so that when I open the lid, Mr. van der Lee, they will rise up like fire, and shoot out of the box like a flame, and that will delight me, Mr. van der Lee, and will remind me of that other fire that one day rose up inside me.

AUTHOR'S NOTE

Insect Dreams is a work of the imagination, an invention, and although the foundation of the novella is based in fact, it should not be taken as a realistic account or considered to be solely what is thought of as historical fiction. Inspired by the life and work of the seventeenth century artist and entomologist, Maria Sibylla Merian (particularly by the two-year period she spent in Surinam studying the insects there), the novella is a poetic rather than an historical rendering, and in that sense strives to draw closer to the soul or spirit of its material than to a factual unfolding of events. Maria Sibylla Merian did live from 1647 to 1717, and did leave the city of Amsterdam in the year 1699 to travel by ship to Surinam, essentially unescorted (a bold act for a woman at that time). She did go into the jungle to conduct her work; she did get malaria; she did encounter and was appalled by the conditions of slavery under the Dutch; she did cut short her stay. These are the facts that serve as the bones of the piece, but the flesh on the bones is imagined. With the exception of Maria Sibylla Merian, all the characters and specific situations have been invented. The italicized communications that begin with the word "Sirs" written to the Amsterdam Naturalists have also been invented. As has the long letter at the end to Mathew van der Lee. The first four sentences of that letter, however, were borrowed from Maria Sibylla Merian's correspondence concerning the settling of her business accounts, and were then recast.

---

[1] Maria Sibylla Merian was in fact accompanied by her daughter on the actual trip to Surinam, which can hardly be viewed as being escorted, especially in the year 1699. She had left her husband some years prior in 1685, also a bold act for a woman of that time.

ABOUT THE AUTHOR

Rosalind Palermo Stevenson's fiction and prose poetry have appeared in anthologies and literary journals including: *Trampoline* (Small Beer Press), *First Intensity, Web Conjunctions, Spinning Jenny, Italian Americana, Skidrow Penthouse, River City,* and *Washington Square,* among others. Her story, "The Guest" was selected as *Italian Americana's* best story of 2005 and was awarded the annual Anne and Henry Paolucci fiction prize for Italian-American writing. Her fiction and prose poems have received several Pushcart nominations. She lives in New York City.